SpongeBob SquarePants®

My Trip to ATLANTiS
by SpongeBob SquarePants

adapted by Sarah Willson
based on the teleplay
"Atlantis SquarePantis" by Dani Michaeli and Steven Banks
illustrated by The Artifact Group

Ready-to-Read

Simon Spotlight/Nickelodeon
New York   London   Toronto   Sydney

Stephen Hillenburg

Based on the TV series *SpongeBob SquarePants*® created by Stephen Hillenburg
as seen on Nickelodeon®

SIMON SPOTLIGHT
An imprint of Simon & Schuster Children's Publishing Division
1230 Avenue of the Americas, New York, New York 10020

Manufactured in the United States of America
8 10 9
Library of Congress Cataloging-in-Publication Data
Willson, Sarah.
My trip to Atlantis (by Spongebob SquarePants) / by Sarah Willson ;
illustrated by The Artifact Group. – 1st ed.
p. cm. – (Ready-to-read ; #12)
"Based on the TV series SpongeBob SquarePants created by Stephen
Hillenburg as seen on Nickelodeon."
ISBN-13: 978-1-4169-3794-4
ISBN-10: 1-4169-3794-3
0111 LAK
I. Artifact Group. II. SpongeBob SquarePants (Television program)
III. Title.
PZ7.W6845My 2007
2007011723

It all began when I was blowing
bubbles with Patrick.
"Watch this, Patrick," I said.
I blew and blew. My bubble was huge!
But then it closed in around us and
began to float away—with us inside!

"Aaaah! What have I done?" I cried.

We floated for a long time.

We finally ended up in a cave.

That's when we heard a *pop*!

The bubble popped on something sharp!

"What is that? It looks like
an old coin," I said.
It looked ancient,
so we decided to take it to
the Bikini Bottom Museum.

We met Sandy and Squidward there.
"Where did you get that?"
Squidward asked.
"This old coin?" I said.
"That's the missing half of the
Atlantian amulet!" said Squidward.

We had no idea what he meant.
"Missing omelet?" asked Patrick.
"No, *amulet*! It is from the lost
city of Atlantis!" Squidward said.
Then he showed us a mural
of Atlantis on the wall.

"They say the streets of Atlantis
   are paved in gold," said Squidward.
"What?" yelled Mr. Krabs.
   He had just appeared out of nowhere!

Squidward told us that Atlantis was
known for its arts and sciences.
"They invented weapons, too.
But the people of Atlantis were
peaceful and never used them,"
he said.

"What's that bubble doing there?"
  I asked Squidward.
"That's the world's oldest bubble.
  The real bubble is in Atlantis."

Then Sandy had an idea.

"Connect the two halves!" she said.

"They might take us to Atlantis!"

So Squidward put them together.

There was a loud *boom*!

Then we saw bright beams of light.

All of a sudden a van appeared!
The amulet floated over to it
and clicked into place.
"All aboard!" said Sandy.
Zoom! We were flying!
We flew and flew until—*crash*!
We were finally there!

We saw a great big palace.

"Welcome to Atlantis!" a man said.

"I am King Lord Royal Highness."

"I am SpongeBob," I said.

"These are my friends."

"Would you care for a tour
    of our great city?" he asked.

We all said yes, and off we went!

"For centuries we have been experts
in art, science, weapons, and
treasure collecting," said the king.
Mr. Krabs jumped up and down.
"I love treasures!" he said.

So the king took us to the
treasure room.
"Help yourself!" he told Mr. Krabs.
We left Mr. Krabs there.
Patrick and I just wanted to see
the world's oldest bubble.

Then Sandy asked to see
the Hall of Inventions.
The Atlantians had invented a lot!
They even had a machine that turned
everything into ice cream!
We left Sandy there to explore.
We kept looking for the bubble.

Squidward wanted to see the art.
We left him in the Hall of Arts.
Finally, I blurted out,
"Please, oh please, may we see
the ancient bubble?"
The king smiled. "Of course!"

"Behold our most beloved treasure,"
the king said.
"This bubble is more than one million
years old. Please be careful!"
The king left. We just stared.
"This is the most beautiful,
wrinkled-up old bubble
I have ever seen!" I said.

Patrick thought so too.
He decided to take a picture
of us with the bubble.

Click! Pop!
"Pat, did you hear something?"
Patrick and I looked at each other.
"Oh, no!" we both yelled.

"We destroyed the most ancient,
priceless treasure in Atlantis!
How will we tell the king?" I asked.

That evening at our dinner feast
we told the king about the bubble.
He just laughed.
"That's not the real bubble.
This is!" he said, showing it off.
But then Patrick took a picture of
the real bubble.
And this one popped too!

"We are so sorry!" I cried out.

The king's face just darkened.

"Guards!" he yelled.

"Do not let them get away!"

"RUN!" shouted Sandy.

We ran and ran.

The guards chased after us.

We ran straight into Plankton.
He was driving a huge tank.
"Cower before me!" he said
with an evil laugh. "Now I have
the most powerful weapon!
Prepare to taste my wrath!"

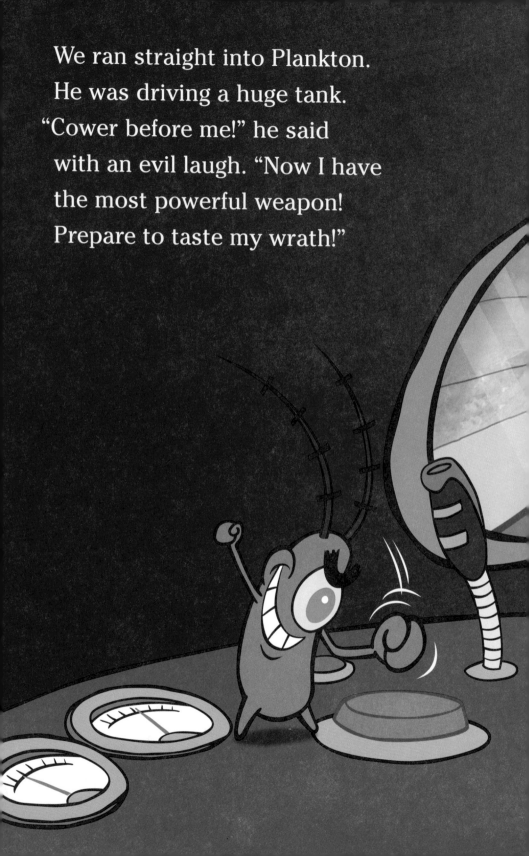

He pressed the button.
I was so afraid!
Splat!

25

"Plankton's wrath tastes like
 ice cream!" said Patrick.
"Mmm!" I said, shoveling it into my mouth.

"This thing blasts ICE CREAM?"
said Plankton angrily.
He climbed down and began
to kick the tank.
"OW!" he yelled.

We were happy that we were saved from Plankton, but we knew the king was still angry with us.

But then the king smiled.
"Look! A talking speck!" he said.
"It will make a great replacement
   for our ruined national treasure."
"I will get you!" yelled Plankton
   as the king picked him up.
"Yes, this is much better than our
   dusty old bubble," he said.

We got back in the van.

We waved good-bye to the king.

He seemed so happy that we had come!

And that whole bubble thing
worked out in the end too.
Boy, Atlantis sure is a great place!

31

We waved good-bye to Plankton.
I hope he has as much fun in Atlantis
as we did!